Jasper's Beanstalk

Nick Butterworth and Mick Inkpen

Hodder
Children's
Books

a division of Hodder Headline Limited

On Monday
Jasper found
a bean.

On Tuesday
he planted it.

On Wednesday
he watered it.

On Thursday
he dug and raked
and sprayed and
hoed it.

On Friday night he picked

up all the slugs and snails.

On Saturday
he even mowed it!

On Sunday
Jasper waited
and waited
and waited…

When Monday
came around again
he dug it up.

'That bean
will never make
a beanstalk,'
said Jasper.

But a   long   long

long   time   later...

It did!

(It was on a Thursday, I think.)

Now Jasper is looking for giants!

British Library Cataloguing in Publication data

A catalogue record for this book is available from the British Library

ISBN 0 340 58634 6

First published 1992 by Hodder Children's Books
Paperback edition first published 1993
16   17   18   19   20

Published by Hodder Children's Books,
a division of Hodder Headline Limited, 338 Euston Road, London NW1 3BH

Printed in Hong Kong